THE MOOR

(BOOK ONE)

Reina Donovan

consult a licensed professional before attempting any techniques outlined in this book.

By reading this document, the reader agrees that under no circumstances are is the author responsible for any losses, direct or indirect, which are incurred as a result of the use of information contained within this document, including, but not limited to, — errors, omissions, or inaccuracies.

TABLE OF CONTENTS

INTRODUCTION

It was the dead of night. The cold darkness stole the warmth from the heart of Gabriella. She almost thought of turning back and getting back into her cozy bed. But, she knew her favorite cousin was waiting for her and he was doing this despite not being fully convinced because of her desires.

Gabriella stole through the long verandah of her magnificent mansion looking over her shoulder to see if anyone is there. It was a new moon night and there was nothing except deathly darkness all around. Her heart was palpitating crazily. She had never thought it would come to this. But, she had no choice. Her parents refused to give in.

She was forced to run! She was not born to live without a bigger purpose than to be a good wife to another rich man (maybe even richer than her parents) and simply bear him children. She was not born to knit and sew and merely entertain other rich guests of her husband's (whoever he maybe). She was not born to die of boredom.

She, Gabriella, was born for greater things. She was born to fight. She was born to kill the plunderers of her beloved Mordo. She was sent to be the princess of Mordo so that she could spare her kingdom from the pains of the Moors who had been plundering it for the last 500 years! She was born to take an active part in the Second Crusades called by His Holiness, the Pope. She was born to kill anyone who dared to slur Christians and Christianity.

But her parents thought differently. They believed a woman's rightful place was next to her husband looking after his home and bearing him children while he went and fought in wars. Her mother tried to convince her of her foolhardy thought and told her that a woman's heart once trapped in a man's heart will never find its way out. Love had the power to control a woman. But love did not have the power to control a man!

And so here she was, in the dead of night when everyone else was sleeping, trying to flee with her cousin from her mother's side, Prince Ralph of Gascoigne, Mordo's neighbor. As promised, her dear cousin Ralph was ready by the riverbank with her favorite mare, Constantine. She quickly climbed on and along with Ralph galloped off into the dead of night.

As she turned and looked at her beautiful home, the Castle of Mordo, she suddenly felt a sense of fear and uncertainty. The round towers seemed to give her some kind of warning. The cross over the chapel appeared to be frowning down upon her. And then she remembered that she wanted to go to the chapel and pray before she left home. She had wanted to ask for forgiveness for causing pain to her parents. But in her hurry, she completely forgot! Now, it was too late to go back. And she was too excited about the adventures that lay ahead of her!

CHAPTER 1

HAROUN

Haroun watched Peasant Rafe sauntering down the alleyway after taking one drop too many to drink. He stealthily follows him knowing fully well that his bronzed facial features will not be seen by anyone on the new moon night. Being the efficient killer he was, Haroun chose this night for his deadly deed.

After all, the moonlight can help people recognize him if they do manage to see him commit his crime. Not that the death of Peasant Rafe will stir anyone to action. Yet, Haroun was trained to be efficient and so he was.

As Peasant Rafe sauntered ahead, Haroun picked up speed and very soon caught up with the drunken man. He drew close and tripped him. Catching him as Rafe fell down because of the tripping, Haroun very efficiently slit his throat in one swift motion. Rafe did not even realize that he was dying and it did not even get the time to scream in agony as he was dead almost instantaneously! Slowly dropping the corpse onto the pavement and wiping off the few drops of Rafe's blood on the floor of the pavement, Haroun continued walking as if the kill was a mere inconvenience.

He walked about two miles before he reached the meeting point where he was paid for his deed. He took the money, did not bother to receive or give thanks, and went his way. Haroun was a trained assassin. He killed for money. He did not take any sides based on any other kind of morals except the moral of economy and commerce. He worked for whoever paid him!

Haroun walked into a tavern at the end of the city and bought himself some food. He always avoided ale on the day he committed the crime. He needed his wits around in case something went wrong and he had to escape or fight those who came to take revenge, if ever.

He bit into the bread and drank the hot bone soup. As he was having his dinner, he overheard some casual conversation at another table.

"Where's Rafe tonight?" asked one man.

"Don't know and don't care!" replied another.

"Heard his wife is been whoring around with some big man in the castle and Rafe found out about it and has kept her prisoner in their home?"

"Pity! She was a sight for sore eyes. Big eyes! Big breasts! Would have loved to have her whoring with me," guffawed the other fellow.

Paying no heed to this, Haroun's thoughts, as is wont when he was alone, went back to his childhood. He was born into a rich Moor family which could trace its origins back to Tangiers when his grandfather thrice or four times removed came to Andalusia in an effort to spread Islam.

The Moors became so powerful and widespread that at one point in time, their kingdom extended to the Pyrenees to the far north of the Iberian Peninsula. Haroun's family moved from strength to strength and become one of the closest families to the Muslim royal family. The future generations of Haroun's family continued to flourish in Medieval Spain as they learned to blend with the local community as much as possible although they kept their religion and rituals as true to the original as possible. Yet the Moors were treated with respectful fear as their temper and viciousness and passion for remorseless violence were famed all over Andalusia.

Although his ancestors made a lot of wealth and lived a life of luxury, when Haroun was born, his family was on its downward slide and riches and wealth were only spoken of as history. His father wasted his life drinking away the last of the family money and lived merely on past glory. There was little love for his father, Haroun thought to himself. "May his soul rot in hell!"

Now, Haroun's mother Ariana was his mentor! She came from an illustrious Moor family too and was very proud of her ancestry. She taught Haroun warring and fighting skills. She always said, "Remember you are a Moor! A powerful and strong Moor! Born to rule! Never bow your head to anyone but the Lord above!"

When his father passed away, Haroun actually heaved a sigh of relief. He was happy that there would be no more beatings and curses to take from the vile man. But, unluckily for Haroun, his mother followed her husband sooner than both of them would have liked and Haroun was an orphan at the tender age of ten!

There were numerous uncles and aunts and cousins in the large, rambling, and dilapidated family castle that was held up only because of pity from God above (as He did not want to wipe out an entire Moor family at once). At least this is what Haroun thought as the walls became unbearably damp during the winters and rainy season and the number of gaping holes in the roof allowed for more water to fall inside the castle than outside when it rained heavily.

He left home a week after his mother passed away. He told himself, "There is nothing for me there now!"

He took shelter in a tavern on the outskirts of the city. He lived here doing odd jobs for the tavern owner in return for food and accommodation. Food was in the form of leftovers and accommodation was under the tables after the tavern closed for the day. His day began at the crack of dawn and he worked till his feet fell sore till past midnight curling up under one of the tables when the tavern doors closed. Yet, he did not complain because he loved this sense of new-found independence.

One day, two hefty men walked into the tavern and placed their orders for alcohol.

"Two large!" cried one and the other pushed and shoved a man sitting quietly with his drink at a nearby table and forcibly sat down at the now empty table. The fallen man picked himself up and walked away without a comment although Haroun did notice a gleam of something in his eyes. The partner guffawed at this scene and sat down heavily on a chair too next to his friend.

The tavern owner's daughter served them the drinks while they leered at her. She was used to this and hence she ignored them and started walking away after filling their cups. But, they started needling her. She yelled at them with some chaste obscenities. This angered them and one of them came lunging toward the girl. Just when everyone present thought the girl was going to get badly hurt, the big man fell down with blood oozing around his throat. He was so fast that no one even saw the quiet man who had walked away earlier, come right in time to slash the throat of the leerer!

People only saw the result; the big hefty man lying slumped down, quite dead, and the quiet man standing over the corpse, his eyes quite remorseless. There was deathly silence all around and only

Haroun seemed to have noticed the partner lunge forward ready with belligerent rage to attack the killer with a deadly knife!

"Look out!" Haroun screamed. That day, Haroun's life took a turn as he saved the quiet man's life. Because, even before he screamed, he took one of the serrated hunting knives hanging on the wall of the tavern and drove it right through the big man's heart. Haroun was lucky that his hand reached right at the center of the big bully's heart. He had no time to react as his heart stopped beating immediately. The scream escaped Haroun an instant after he lunged forward! Now, the other partner lay as dead as the first man!

The quiet man walked out of the tavern as if this kill was a mere inconvenience! Haroun stared after him and as he walked out the door, he beckoned to the boy! Haroun walked toward him mesmerized by the entire scene, his little yet powerful hands bloodied with the blood of a man he just killed. The quiet killer held Haroun's hand and led him out! They walked over to a stream that flowed nearby. He helped Haroun wash off the blood from his hands.

"You have skills! Do you want to use them and see the world?"

Haroun dumbly nodded. "Follow me," he said. That was the last Haroun saw of the tavern which was his home for nearly a year!

The following two years was spent in the company of the quiet killer whose name was Sancho. He was part of a gang of pirates. He became a father figure to Haroun, something his original father was never able to be.

He taught Haroun his skill and trade which was that of an assassin. The Moor learned the different ways to kill, how to use the different kinds of knives. He learned to kill by stealth. He learned to kill openly. He learned that killing others allowed him to live and live well. He learned to sail from the pirate gang and he learned to read and interpret the ways of the seas! Haroun and his pirate gang plundered and looted and killed and made more money than he had dreamed of.

The fame of Haroun's skill spread far and wide and people who killed for money efficiently seemed to be in short supply. Work never ceased! The little boy who was now a strapping and powerful young man traveled across Andalusia doing his job as efficiently as possible and with each kill, he gained more wealth.

Now, this was a time in Andalusia when Christian uprising swelled against the Moors. Haroun's skill was needed both by the Moors and the Christians and he took no sides except the side of money. Haroun worked for whoever paid him more. So, sometimes, he was a soldier in the Christian army against the Moors and, sometimes, he was in the army of the Moors against the Christians.

He also worked for people who hired him to take care of troublesome people in their lives. That was the job he just accomplished by killing Peasant Rafe. He never asked for reasons why someone wanted to kill someone else. If he got paid, he killed. He was a popular killer as his ability to use his skills was matched by no one in the whole of Andalusia! Yet, h had to be careful because the victims' family could be searching for him to take revenge. And Haroun had definitely had made far more than his share of enemies.

CHAPTER 2
GABRIELLA

Gabriella was the beloved daughter of Lord Esmour Martyn of Mordo. Being the only child and surrounded by a male cousins, Lord Esmour lavished love and affection on her. Gabriella's mother, Lady Irene, was the daughter of the highly respected and illustrious king of Galuven descended from one of the Templar Knights going back many generations. Gabriella was brought up in luxury as should be a princess of high standing.

She was highly influenced by the Catholic Church to which both her parents belonged. However, her royalty combined with a strict Catholic upbringing did little to stymie Gabriella's rebellious streak. While she was a devout Catholic she was very headstrong and believed in feminine power. She openly criticized many of the customs of her times which made women subjugated under a man.

"Why should I be under the thumb of anyone?" she asked of her mother. Her fiery eyes lit up her beautiful face and the blueness in her eyes seemed swallowed by the golden fire that they emanated when she felt slighted by such formalities. Gabriella insisted on learning all the things her male cousins and brothers learned.

She took fencing, sword-fighting, and horse-riding lessons. And she was so good at them that in the many duels that she had with her cousins, she came out easily victorious. Her favorite cousin was Ralph who was her constant companion and was very understanding of her rebellious nature. In fact, he encouraged her to be independent and taught her a lot more skills of a warrior than was allowed for a woman in those days.

While Lord Esmour adored his daughter blindly, Gabriella's mother was stricter with her. She admonished her for her brazenness and warned her of consequences that she will not be able to bear if she chose to rebel to such an extent. She tried to teach Gabriella knitting and sewing. But the stubborn girl refused to learn.

Her refusal had nothing to do with her incapability but a lot of do with the fact that activities like knitting and sewing were lady-like and she did not want to be anything lady-like. She really abhorred being told to do anything against her will.

Yet, Gabriella was a devoted Catholic and attended Bible classes regularly. In these classes, she learned about the Crusades and the stories of brave knights and warriors fighting to keep her religion free from foreign invaders and influences drove her deep desire to be part of the Crusades.

But her mother would hear none of it. And in this regard, her doting father supported her mother wholeheartedly.

"I can't live at home in peace knowing that my dear daughter is facing dangers in the war. Anyway, those hardships are for men. You just look pretty and have a rich life filled with luxuries. Have plenty of children and shower them with love like how your mother does and how her mother did before her! I only gave in to your whim of wanting to learn to fight so that you can save yourself if in a quandary! Not to run off to fight the Crusades!" he said.

Deeply disappointed by the turn of events, Gabriella hatched a plan. She had heard of Captain Philip who was in Mordo recruiting knights for the Crusades. She was going to join his army whether her parents gave her permission or not!

However, Gabriella was smart enough to know that she will need help and who else could she turn to but her trusted cousin, Ralph?

"You are completely mad!" This was Ralph's initial reaction at her running off idea. But slowly Gabriella convinced him of her strength of resolve in this matter and that she was not doing this because she wanted to prove something but because it was a calling. She was born into this family so that she could fight for its safe upkeep. Otherwise, she would not have felt this deep urge to do leave her loving parents, especially her doting father, and run off into unknown dangers. Ralph was convinced a little. But his love for his cousin was the bigger reason he was willing to take the risk. Gabriella understood this.

So, the day when the two cousins planned to run dawned bright and clear. Captain Philip was stationed about 50 miles away from Mordo and she needed about two to three days to reach him. She surreptitiously packed food and clothing for her journey. Ralph was to meet her at the riverbank with her mare, Constantine and they were both going to flee.

Things went according to plan and the day after their escape, the two royals were about 25 miles away from Mordo. They were in the middle of a lush green forest the beauty of it only being broken by occasional sounds of wild beasts. Sometimes, Gabriella thought she heard the growling sounds of bears. Despite being a strong person who is not easily scared, the Princess of Mordo did find her hair standing on edge at these wild sounds coming from different parts of the thick dense forests.

The two of them stopped only for meals and to wash themselves of grime and dirt. During the night, Ralph pitched tents he had brought. Ralph spoke very little during the journey and Gabriella attributed this to his sense of fear and uncertainty which were the emotions that she was going through as well. So, she too stayed to herself, kept her thoughts to herself, and spoke very little. Yet, Ralph was more nervous than was necessary, she thought.

After all, the plan was perfect. Ralph had pretended to leave for his castle about two days before and he had stayed with an uncle unknown to everyone else. He wanted to return to his kingdom as he was not as keen as her to join the Crusades. So, they plotted a plan where he will help Gabriella and yet be able to return home.

Everyone at Mordo thought Ralph was in Gascoigne and he had people there who would verify his story including the uncle who lived in Mordo and had a home in Gascoigne as well. After ensuring that Gabriella was safely ensconced with Captain Philip, Ralph would return home and pretend surprise at the absence of Gabriella. She thought it was a foolproof plan and they had worked out the details quite so that there would not be a problem for him. Still, why was he so worried?

"Ralph, I am sorry I dragged you into this. But can you please relax now that things are going fine." Gabriella said before retiring to her tent the second night. He just scowled at her and this really did surprise her. Ralph had never scowled at her before. He must be worried about something.

She was too headstrong a woman to allow someone else to take undue discomfort for her sake. So, she told him, "Listen Ralph. I completely understand the anger you are feeling toward me. I am truly grateful for what you have done for me till now. I think I will be able to manage from here. Why don't you return to Gascoigne as planned from here itself?"

Ralph looked at her mysteriously and his eyes gleamed. But he said nothing. He just turned and went into his tent and pulled down the flap shutting her out of his world. Gabriella was amazed how someone whom she trusted and cared for and who trusted and cared for her in equal measure could suddenly become a stranger? Maybe, it was the effects of the strange jungle.

She went to bed with a heavy heart not sure at all if she can manage without Ralph. But, she was certain about her next step. She would get up before dawn and go away without Ralph. "I am being too much of a burden on him and I don't think it's fair!"

She lay down on her mattress made of leaves and thought of her luxurious bed at home. Strangely she did not miss the luxury. But, she did miss the attention and love that she was showered with at home. She lay back and thought of her beautiful castle at Mordo.

CHAPTER 3

THE CASTLE OF MORDO

While Gabriella spent her first night outside of the Castle of Mordo, she couldn't help remembering each detail of the stupendous structure that was her home. She knew every nook and corner of the castle and she had walked the myriad underground maze of tunnels and dungeons a thousand times. She enjoyed every trip with her father into the maze and she came away astounded by the labyrinthine tunnels. She became so well-versed with them that she could hide for days on end without being found except if she wanted to be found!

Her mind raced through the various parts of the castle which was her home until yesterday. She knew that she would go back to it victorious in her efforts to slay the marauders invaders. But for now, it remained only in her thoughts.

Her thoughts traced the innumerable arrow loops found across the outer walls which were built to shoot arrows at the oncoming enemy army while remaining safe within the walls of the castle. She could almost feel the smoothness of the Ashlar blocks that were used to build the entire rambling castle.

In her mind, she ran through the 25 different baileys spread across the castle surrounded by walls that kept the inmates safe. There were baileys in the upper deck, in the lower deck, on the east side, and on the west side. These baileys were the favorite playgrounds for her and her cousins. She would undergo her fencing, sword-fighting, and horse-riding trainings here.

She thought of the stately barbican that housed the guards who kept watch over the gates of the castle. She had stayed with old Stephen in the barbican many times when he stood guard and told her innumerable battle stories. She remembered the hundreds of times she raced with her cousins all around the barmkin. Invariably, she was one of the very few who did not get breathless even when she ran around the barmkin hundreds of times.

She remembered the number of times she climbed up till the bartizan and the bastion to get a bird's eye view of entire Mordo. She loved to look at her kingdom from this height. How many times she had pictured herself ensconced in one of the battlements in imaginary battles that she fought with an oncoming Moor army.

One of her favorite haunts of Castle Mordo was the large courtyard where she played, trained, and spent a lot of happy times with her cousins. She loved to look at the drawbridge each time it was raised or lowered and whenever she heard the sound of its movement, she would run across to the vantage point to watch the drawbridge being lowered and raised. She loved listening to the sounds the drawbridge as the guards used the lever mechanism to pull it up or lower it down.

Gabriella loved leaning over the embrasures and many times her father had come running to her scared that if she leaned too much over then she could slip over the wall! She loved to scare him like this and always used this trick to get him to come to her and give her one of his warm hugs. The hallway was one of her favorites too. She loved the chandeliers hanging all over and always helped the servant light them up whenever she could. She loved the way the servants pulled the rope once all the candles were light and her eyes gleamed as she saw the lit-up chandelier rise up to the roof!

Another favorite place was the moat. She enjoyed the swishing of the water in the moat and she loved to feed the huge crocodiles there. She knew no one dared enter the castle by trying to swim through the moat. The crocodiles were lying in wait to have such people for their supper. The depth of the moat was also capable of sending shivers down the spines of the best swimmers.

Although during her lifetime, the murder hole was never used, she had heard lots of stories from old Stephen while she talked with him in the barbican. Huge balls of fire would be thrown through these murder holes to kill incoming besiegers. The Castle of Mordo was highly protected.

Gabriella loved to look through the trelliswork of the oriel windows spread all across the castle. She would press her face on the trelliswork and feel the designs being etched onto her skin. She cherished that feel. She had once tried to take a peek into the oubliette to see the prisoners who were held captive there. But, her father took this very seriously and he refused to talk to her till she promised that she would never try to do this again. And Gabriella has stuck to her promise. She never tried to get into the oubliette.

She cherished those moments in the castle when she and Ralph would quietly sneak out through the postern to spend some time in the thick jungle behind and splashed in the cool waters of a spring nearby. She remembered once trying to push open the Yett and finding it impossible for it to move even by a hair's breath. It needed the strength of four elephants to push open the Yett when needed.

Her world revolved around the Castle of Mordo. She knew of no other world except that of Mordo. And yet, the heroic stories of the Crusaders filled her with a desire to see and take part in the Crusades. As these thoughts flew past her head, she got drowsy and fell asleep into a dream of Crusades and knights and warriors. Her soft mattress at home was replaced by uncomfortable leaves and bark. And yet, she felt a strange sense of anticipation. Like her life was going to change drastically.

"I have to be ready to sacrifice if I choose to work for Him," she thought and fell asleep.

She was dreaming that she was fighting in the Crusades and Captain Philip was very happy. She was fencing with enemy warriors and chasing them out of her precious land. She was staring into the dark eyes of the most handsome man she had ever seen and suddenly she realized that the last thing was not a dream.

There was this handsome man with rippling muscles and intense dark eyes staring into her. She stared back with wonder for a long time before she realized that a serrated knife fell off from his right hand and nearly struck her leg. She jumped up and screamed. The man simply let go of her and only then she realized that she was cradled in his arms and their faces were as close to each other as was possible for two human faces to be!

CHAPTER 4

THE MEETING

A fter he dropped her, Gabriella lay on her makeshift mattress for a little while completely mesmerized by the face that was looking down on her. She then spotted the knife and gingerly picked it up. It was a thing of beauty. Its dark-brown wooden handle was carved beautifully and the serrated edges were really sharp.

She just touched it and immediately drew her hand back as it seared her skin and a drop of blood oozed out. She was too amazed at the turn of events. She got up and went outside the tent. There was no sign of the man. Who was he? Why was he in her tent? Was he a tribal who was looking to rob? Strangely, she felt no fear! She only felt a peculiar kind of warmth in her heart that was completely new to her!

Calling out for Ralph, she approached his tent and peered in. He was not there. Did he flee after the intruder? Anyway, she thought that this intruder episode suited her plans well. It was time for her to move on without Ralph. She hoped to reach Captain Philip's army by evening and so she abandoned her tent and simply left with a small satchel of food and her water bag.

She climbed onto her Constantine and prodded her on towards Captain Philip. She would have traveled for about an hour and a part of her heart wanted to see Ralph coming for her. Another part wanted to see that handsome face again. She thought she had forgotten about the intruder but his dark intense eyes refused to leave her thoughts. She felt that some part of her was left behind in those eyes.

"Who was the man? And why do I feel so strange about him? After all, he seemed to have come to either rob or, perhaps, even rape her? Then why did she not feel anger or resentment against him? What thoughts were running behind those intense eyes that seemed to probe deep into her soul?" These uncomfortable thoughts raced through her mind as she rode towards Captain Philip and his Crusading Army.

As she moved ahead, she continued to hear the sounds of various wild animals and despite her sense of confidence, she was scared. But, she refused to give in to her fears and galloped on.

Suddenly, through the trees, came three masked men who pounced on Gabriella dropping her off her horse. She was shaken only for a moment. She immediately jumped on to her feet and took out her sword and started fighting the bandits off. The men were quite surprised to see such agility in a woman and they did not expect this at all. One of three men fell down wounded badly.

The other two lunged forward together and Gabriella knew that she would not be able to handle them on her own. She now thought of her parents and said to herself, "Maybe this is the end!" But, she will not go down without a fight. She fought valiantly but the men were not bandits without training. Both struck together and her sword flew from her hands and fell some distance away. She quickly took out her small knife and struck one of the two men on his thigh. He screamed in pain. But, the agony only angered him further and with the help of his partner pinned Gabriella down on the ground.

The men leered as they began tearing bits and pieces of her clothing. She felt quite helpless. But she knew this was not how she wanted her life to end. She wanted to die fighting in the Crusades not raped by bandits in the forest!

At this point in time, out of the blue, two arrows came in such rapid succession that the two men fell over each other in a heap without even realizing what hit them. The arrowheads had pierced the center of their hearts!

Gabriella got up and hastily arranged her clothing and looked in the direction from where the arrows came. She found the same pair of intense dark eyes staring back at her! She gasped as she watched the man come out from his hiding place and walk towards her! The muscles in his hands and legs were rippling with energy and his demeanor made it appear that he did everything with incredible ease.

He walked towards Gabriella and she continued to stare at him completely under his spell. He too seemed to be in some kind of spell as he moved towards her. When they were close enough, he simply bent down and kissed her full on her lips and she too simply responded to the thrill of his kiss. She kissed him back and when they drew away from each other after a while, they were both breathless.

"Who are you?" she managed to ask. He did not respond. Instead, he lifted her and put her on her horse and told her, "I will come with you till Captain Philip's army where you will be safe from raping marauders!"

They rode together for some time and he picked juicy fruits for her! He watched her while she ate and simply did not understand what he felt for her. He had had many women and never had he felt for anyone the way he was feeling for Gabriella.

She was supposed to be his next kill. Her cousin, Ralph, had paid him a substantial amount to kill her. Ralph had told him of her plans to join the Crusades. He had pre-planned the route they were going to take and told him to waylay her on the way and slit her throat. As was his norm, Haroun did not bother to find out the reason. He only made sure that Ralph made the advance payment and had followed both of them from the outskirts of Mordo.

As he followed them waiting for her to get into a relaxed state before attacking, he found her ways very intriguing. Here was a rich woman who could have anything she wanted and yet, she was running away to fight the Crusades!! Wow, how many women happily exchange places with her? And she was going n the reverse direction!

"Anyway, what do I care? I will do my job and then move on to the next," he had told himself as he followed her and watched her from a distance.

Then, on the second night of the journey, when she had settled in to her tent, Ralph and he met and decided that now the time was ripe. Ralph left for his home knowing well that there is no way Haroun is going to miss his victim. He has never missed any victim till now! So, why would he miss killing Gabriella? Ralph decided not to wait for the macabre event to actually take place and see the dead body of his cousin. He just decided to go home to give his uncle the good news.

Haroun stealthily crept into Gabriella's tent, his serrated knife ready in his right hand. He looked down at Gabriella and suddenly, something clicked. He looked into that beautiful face and he knew he would never be the same again. All his training was a complete waste. He could not bring himself to lift his right hand and slit her throat. Instead, he put his left hand under her neck and gently lifted her face. He wanted to kiss her! At that moment, she opened her eyes and they were the most brilliant blue he had ever seen! He felt his heart lurch and the knife fall from his hand.

He knew he had fallen in love at that moment. He knew that he would do everything in his power to keep his love safe. The only thing he felt saddened about at that time was the fact that it is most unlikely that she will love him back.

Then, suddenly today, when this event with bandits happened. He had been following her since she left the tent after finding Ralph's tent empty. He followed her this time not to kill but to keep her safe. The wild animals were not as much a problem as bandits, he knew.

Haroun knew of the deadly Three Killers gang was somewhere in the vicinity. He realized that they must have, by now, seen the young beautiful princess wandering the forest alone. They will not let go of such an easy prey. To save her from bandits is why he chose to follow Gabriella.

And they came and lunged at her. Haroun was about to rush to her aid when he saw with what amazing agility Gabriella got onto her feet and wounded one of three men! He watched her move with speed and accuracy swishing her sword and attacking her attackers fearlessly. Haroun had never met a woman like her! Now, he was truly and irretrievably in love with Gabriella.

Despite her attempts, the two remaining men were onto her like animals. At that point, he let go of two arrows that pierced their hearts like in the center. Then, he watched her blue eyes scan the area and rest on him. Now, he was truly overcome. He walked out of his hiding place and went to her and kissed her.

To his surprise, she kissed him back with passion! He was bewitched beyond reason. Was she smitten too? "Oh, I wish the pain in my heart stopped and I knew for sure she was in love with me as much as I was!"

They broke away and were breathlessly looked at each other. Then, getting his wits back, Haroun lifted her and put her on her horse. She asked him who he was. He couldn't bring himself to answer her and instead told her that he will accompany her till she reached the safety of Captain Philip.

CHAPTER 5

CHANGE OF PLAN

Around noon, while taking a break from the journey under the shade of a large old tree, Gabriella asked the man (she still did not know his name and she had already kissed him!), "So, what were you doing in my tent? Same thing as the bandit? To ravish me?"

Haroun looked at her and then away. He couldn't meet her eyes because, for the first time in his entire life, he wanted to be someone other than what he was. He wanted to tell Gabriella that he was a builder or a carpenter or a farmer! Anything but a killer! It was indeed strange that he was ashamed to show his true colors to her! Is this what love is? To hide the wrongs and show only the nice thing!

Something stirred within him and he decided to lay bare his life to Gabriella. He started, "My name is Haroun and I am a sword for hire! I kill for money. And this is what I have been doing the past 15 years of my life. Killing for a living!"

Gabriella's blue eyes went bluer and she started from her place and ran helter-skelter. He stayed where he was and made no attempt to pursue her. Gabriella climbed onto her horse and rode away as far as she could from the man she was hopelessly falling in love with! He was a murderer, a killer? And he was a Moor.

Here she was trying to fight against Christian enemies and today, she had given her heart to a Moor? Her mind was in turmoil. She had reached a stream and got off from her horse. Splashing water over her face, hoping that the nightmare she was living was only a nightmare and she would wake up in her warm bed. When she opened her eyes, Haroun was there in front of her and his dark intense eyes seemed to penetrate her soul again. She was hopelessly in love with him. Despite knowing his roots, she wanted to love him.

She reached out and pulled him to her bosom and they held onto each other's love. Haroun looked up at her and said, "I don't know why Gabriella, but I love you and I know that I want you to be by my side till I die!"

Gabriella's eyes lit up with unshed tears and she told him, "Yes, Haroun, I only know your name and I know you are from the enemy camp. Yet, I love you and I know not why too!"

They kissed, first gently. Slowly the kiss became more passionate and they had to literally tear away from each other lest the passions overtook their sense of dignity in the open jungle.

"So, what were you doing in my tent?"

"I was there to kill you!"

"What? Why? We don't even know each other?"

"I told you I was a killer by profession and someone had paid me to kill you."

Gabriella reeled under the impact of this new knowledge! The only person who was aware that she will be in this jungle on this path was Ralph! So, he must have been involved somehow! Why?

She looked to Haroun for help! He seemed as baffled. "I never ask for the reason. I just follow orders once the payment has been made. Yes, it was Ralph who approached me and paid me to murder you. But I do not know why?"

They both sat in silence. Haroun was feeling miserable for putting Gabriella to so much pain. But, he knew he was right in having confessed himself to her. His heart felt freer and he felt he deserved her love more than before. He did not hide who he was and yet she proclaimed her love. There must be some deeper connection between us. For the moment, Haroun was simply happy to revel in his feeling of mutual love.

Gabriella, on the other hand, was having confusing thoughts. Her trusted Ralph wanting to kill her! Why? She thought back to the wonderful times she had spent with her cousin and not a single time did it strike her that he was feeling so much animosity towards her. What had she done? And, in addition to these confusing thoughts, was the overwhelming love she was feeling for this Moor. Why was she so attracted to him? And what was she to do?

Haroun broke into her thoughts, "If you will listen to me, I think I might help you unravel some amount of confusion from your mind. Let us go back to Mordo. You go to your father and confess your guilt for having run away! Yes, he is going to be really angry. But, that is the only way you will know why Ralph wanted you killed. And I now know you can never live in peace until you have an answer for that!"

Gabriella looked at him in wonder. He can read her mind too! Yes, I will never find peace till I know what made Ralph so angry that he wanted me killed! I have to get to the truth of the matter.

So, they turned back and were on the outskirts of Mordo in two days. Haroun stopped her when they had reached the outskirts and told her that he will not come into Mordo. He was after all a Moor and Mordo was a Christian kingdom and he will not be spared. "I now want to live for this love, my beloved." Gabriella also realized the truth in his statement and she knew that it is quite unlikely that there love has a future. Her parents will never agree to let their only daughter be married to a Moor.

They got off from their horses to say their goodbyes. Gabriella was sobbing openly while Haroun's eyes were filled with unshed tears.

They did not kiss but simply hugged each other for some time. Then, he let her go and got onto his horse and rode off back into the jungle.

Gabriella's heart tore to see her beloved's back thinking that this is the last time she will be seeing him. She called out to him silently and he turned back one last time and waved before taking a turn that took him out of her sight.

She rode back to the Mordo castle dejectedly. She knew the space in her chest was empty because her heart had followed Haroun. As she went closer to her home, she found people surrounding her horse and cheering her. Her attempt to join Captain Philip may not have found favor with her parents. But, her people seemed to love her for it. However, they were also curious to know why she returned so early. She promised them that she will give her full story once she reached home and first spoke to her parents.

Word reached the castle before she did and there was a big entourage waiting to receive her joyously. Her father was at the head of the assembly waiting to receive her and he grabbed her in his arms and hugged her shedding copious tears. Her mother hugged her with less fervor and Gabriella knew she was going to have the biggest showdown she had ever had with her mom very soon.

But, that was for later. She looked around for Ralph and did not find him in the crowd. She mentioned nothing about the events in the jungle. She merely told her father that she realized her folly and hence chose to return home. She realized her life's purpose was to serve a Christian knight who will fight in the Crusades while she stayed home and reared his children.

Her father was thrilled to hear about this and immediately announced her marriage to Cousin Ralph. This was not surprising as everyone simply assumed that the friendship between Ralph and Gabriella was more than just platonic and the families of Gascoigne and Mordo were more than happy to see them get married and combine royalty and riches. It would be a perfect political marriage.

Gabriella was taken aback with this announcement. For one, she never felt anything more than a platonic kinship towards Ralph and now this intention of Ralph to get her killed changed even that for her. And, finally, she has given her heart to Haroun and she could not allow anyone to take his place. Yet, she kept quiet hoping to unravel the new mystery around Ralph.

"Where is Ralph?" asked Gabriella.

"Oh! He has gone home to Gascoigne. His parents were here at Mordo in an effort to console your mother. After all, they are her cousins as well! But Ralph is on his way to Mordo."

The betrothal announcement of Gabriella and Ralph called for a celebration and the entire kingdom of Mordo celebrated. The castle rang in the festivities with overflowing wine and feasts. The celebration went late into the night and it was nearly dawn when Gabriella could finally tear herself away from her cousins to speak to her parents.

There was absolutely no sign of Ralph and Gabriella knew exactly why he did not turn up. And she was duty-bound to let her parents know the truth about Ralph.

CHAPTER 6

THE TRUTH

Gabriella went towards her parent's room and before she could knock on the door, she heard her mother say, "The Moor whore!" Gabriella froze.

Then, she heard the sound of a slap ring through and her father's voice said, "Don't you dare call her that?"

"Of course I will call her by her profession. And to think I was forced to look after her daughter as my own. Disgusting!"

"She is my daughter as well. And if I hadn't found Ayesha, I would have been childless because we have not had a child after that, have we?" This was her father talking!

"Yes, maybe not! But we would not be having a half-Moor for a daughter would we?" her mother screamed. "And I will not let her pollute my family by allowing her to marry Ralph!"

Gabriella could not stop herself and she barged into the room and watched in horror as flashes of hatred passed between her parents. She had never seen her parents like this before.

"Who is the Moor Whore and who is this daughter you are talking about," demanded Gabriella.

For an instant, her parents just stared dumbly at her. Then, her father's face fell and he watched in dismay as her mother walked across to his beloved daughter and say, "Your mother is the Moor whore and you are the daughter we were talking about!"

Gabriella was too stunned to say anything. She stood rock-still till her mother reached her and shook her! Gabriella saw her father's fallen face and realized that her mother was telling the truth.

She was in a completely dazed state. She flung herself out of the room, ran across the verandah and took the same path that she took a couple of days ago in her bravado attempt to join the Crusades! And here she was today, unsure of her own identity.

She climbed onto the first horse available and galloped away into the night. She drove like a raging woman and she had no idea where she was going! She just let the horse choose his own route.

Soon, she reached the dense thick forest. Completely enervated, she got off from her horse and sat down under a tree on a protruding root. She tried hard to compose her thoughts. She was not her mother's daughter? Her mother was a Moor whore! Why was her Christian father associated with a Moor? Who was she? A Christian or a Moor? She had no answers and her mind was in a web! She just shed copious tears!

Just then, out of the blue, three masked men came at her! Even in her demented state of mind, she realized that one of these was the same bandit she had wounded earlier. Haroun had saved her from the other two. Today, she realized she did not have Haroun to rescue her. But, she refused to die in this humiliating way. So, she sprung forward and quickly took out the dagger from the belts of one of the bandits. She would kill herself before she allowed any of these wretched creatures touch her.

As she was getting ready to either fight or die fighting, she heard a loud roar and out sprang Haroun from the dense thicket with his sword swirling high. The bandits were taken aback but were not ready to give in. A wounded bandit wanted his revenge. Between Haroun and Gabriella, they fought off the bandits again. Haroun was a trained and skilled warrior. If he could kill for money, he could kill twice as fast for love.

He realized this as he swirled his sword all around and wounded the bandits repeatedly. He saw his beloved Gabriella fighting ferociously as well. He felt his heart swell with pride and love for her and he decided at that very moment that no matter who or what came in the way, he will stick to Gabriella till death do them apart. Soon, the bandits were overwhelmed and took off in fright.

Thoroughly exhausted, Gabriella and Haroun fell into each other's arms and held on dearly till their breathing returned to normal. Then, they stepped back and looked at each other with renewed interest. Haroun was astounded that Gabriella was in the jungle again and Gabriella was astounded that Haroun was still around!

Despite their confusing thoughts, they were so happy to see each other! Holding hands, they sat down under the tree and shared their stories that happened in the few hours that they parted. While Gabriella told him her sad story and how she realized in the last few hours that she might not be the person she believed she was, Haroun told her that he couldn't bring himself to go very far away from her. So, he roamed around in the jungle hoping for some kind of miracle.

He looked at her with loving eyes and said, "It seems like my prayer has been answered!"

She smiled back too. But, her mind was still seeking answers and Haroun decided to help her find the answers. They rode back to town and surreptitiously took a place at a local inn for the night. They slept soundly after a harrowing day and felt refreshed the next morning.

Gabriella needed answers. How to get them? She thought it best to approach her father for help. If her mother was not the real one, she knew that her father was indeed the Lord of Mordo. He would provide her with answers.

So, they waited till dark and then went towards the castle. Gabriella knew the ins and outs of the castle and also knew of its many secret passages that her father had shown to her many times. Instinctively, she used one of these passages and reached a door. She pushed and the door opened. She saw her father sitting on the couch and looking toward the door. He knew she will come back and he had kept the door open. By now, word had spread about the infidelity of the Lord of Mordo and how he had raised a Moor child even though he was her father! It was an unforgivable act and the matter was being taken to the Pope for his judgment. Her father will surely be beheaded, she knew! Such a kind of sacrilege had only death written all over it.

She ran toward her father and hugged him. He hugged her back, sat her down beside her and told her, "You deserve to know the story of your mother and my intense love for her." At this point in time, his eyes fell on Haroun. Gabriella immediately said, "I trust him implicitly, my dear father. Otherwise I would not have brought him here."

The Lord of Mordo had a glint in his eye as he studied Haroun. He smiled at his daughter and said, "Strange are the ways of life!"

He then related the story of the lady who was Gabriella's mother. The Lord of Mordo had met her while fighting the Moors. Her husband was killed in a recent battle and the other men of her tribe were fighting over each other to get her. She was disgusted and had run away. The Lord of Mordo had saved her from a pack of wolves and it was love at first sight for him. She took much longer to reciprocate his love but, finally, she did give in.

He brought her secretly to Mordo and kept in a secluded home far away from the crowded town. She understood the dilemmas that both of them were facing. Their love would be considered sacrilege and they would both be put to death. So, she was willing to live the life of a secluded yet beloved wife of the Lord of Mordo though their marriage was solemnized only by their hearts and not by any priest.

They lived happily like this for about two years and soon, Ayesha, for that was Gabriella's mother's name, was pregnant. But, his father was pressuring him to marry someone eligible and he had to give into the pressures of those times and he married the woman who was his present wife from the Gascoigne family. Ayesha did not complain and knew that he had no option but to go along with the wedding.

"The time for your mother's delivery was drawing close. I had kept some trusted servants with her to help her during her pregnancy. But, it did seem that all was not well with her pregnancy. When the time came, she had a lot of pain and I could hear her screams as I waited in the outside room. The maid came outside after a few hours to tell me that you were born. You know today I realize that the sweetest sound that I have ever heard was the sound of your first cry! My heart swelled with happiness and unbridled joy!"

"But all was not well. Ayesha did not survive the childbirth. Before she died, she begged me to make sure that I give you a good life. In fact, she told me to bring you up as a Christian so you may have no confusions in your mind. She wanted you to marry a Christian and grow up with no enmity."

"But it was hard. Your Moorish roots were very strong. Your mother was a great warrior too and was skilled in sword-fighting and horse-riding and fencing. You carried it in your genes. I chose to let you have what you want because you were a part of my most beloved wife!"

"It was difficult to convince my Christian wife, Lady Irene of Galuven, but I had to. I threatened. I cajoled. I begged. I did everything in my power to convince her to take you as her child. Initially, she was reluctant. But, then she gave in. She had only one condition. No one was to know that the child was Ayesha's. She wanted everyone to believe that the child was hers! This surprised me because that is exactly what I wanted her to do. So, why was she asking as a return favor? That is when she told me about a love affair she had had during her younger wild days and she had gotten pregnant. In her fear, she had got the child aborted. But the procedure was done so badly that she had lost her ability to bear children. And she did not want this story to come out. So, she took on the role of her natural mother while I held her secret with me!"

Gabriella was crying as she heard the story of her parents. Both suffered so much of humiliation to keep her alive and happy. "Why the sudden change in attitude from the Queen?" asked Gabriella. She couldn't bear to call her mother any more.

"I don't know. Perhaps the resentment that she was holding down surfaced when she realized that her family will get a bit of the Moor blood when you married Ralph." This made sense. The mention of Ralph made her realize that she hadn't told her part of the story to her father.

Gabriella narrated her story and the Lord of Mordo felt sick that he was planning to get his beloved daughter married to a murderer. Yet, she did not understand why Ralph wanted her killed.

At that moment, the door opened and in walked Ralph, the Lady of Mordo, and Ralph's uncle who was supposed to have helped her get to Captain Philip.

The Queen's face was contorted in anger and Ralph was whimpering in fear. The uncle was also incredibly angry. "How did you escape from the killer? He never allowed his victims to escape," she screamed in helpless rage.

Haroun, who was in the shadows till now, emerged and on seeing him, the three faces went ashen. "What are you doing here?" blurted out Ralph.

"I came to get Gabriella justice."

The Lord of Mordo realized that it was his wife who had plotted to kill his daughter and in his rage, he lunged forth and drove his dagger through his wife's heart killing her instantly. Nobody got any time to stop this act. Ralph's uncle screamed in agony at seeing the Queen fall dead. His rage drove him towards the Lord of Mordo. But by this time, Haroun was alert and he stopped the uncle with his sword. He pinned him down and tied him to the chair. Ralph was looking on in horror as this scene unfolded. He looked like he would be happy to run away.

But Haroun had closed the door by now. The Lord of Mordo went towards Ralph's uncle and asked him, "Why did you want to kill my daughter?"

His face turned ugly with rage as he looked at Gabriella and said, "That is Moorish filth that is corrupting the Christian world! She had no right to live, leave alone live in luxury. She was becoming very popular with her people as well. She needed to be stopped and so I chose to get her killed. Your wife was completely on my side as she was becoming quite tired of your untiring love towards your concubine's daughter!"

49

The Lord of Mordo fell in a heap and turned to Gabriella and said, "My dear, run away from this place that has no place for love. Go with your Moor man and find your heaven of love. No one will ever understand love in Mordo where people prefer killing each other rather than loving each other."

'Take her away, Haroun. Her Moor roots have found her. Fate has a way with us! I tried hard to bring her up as a Christian but not a Christian filled with hatred but a Christian filled with love. Yet, the church she went to taught her to fight the Crusades. But when she met you, she learned to love. She is yours. Take her away while the people of Mordo and those of Gascoigne murder and plunder. Let them fritter this life that God has given them to love by killing and murdering. You take Gabriella away from here. She was not born to kill. She was born to love like her mother!"

CONCLUSION

Ralph came forward and touched Gabriella by her shoulder. She screamed at him, "Don't you dare touch me. Why did you do what you did, Ralph? I thought we were good friends and shared all our thoughts. Why did you do what you did?"

Ralph looked into her forlorn eyes and hated himself. He had betrayed her trust and faith. She had come to him with her deepest desires and he did not realize that.

"Remember the night we ran away together? You asked me why I was so upset despite making preparations for my safe return. I couldn't respond to you nor look at you in your face. That is because if you had seen my face that night, you would have known that something was wrong and you would have gotten it out of me. I left after I met Haroun and showing him your tent knowing fully well that I will not be able to see your dead body."

"But I admit that for some time, I just got carried away by hatred. This man who is my uncle used me and I let him manipulate me into doing the things I did. When I first heard that you were the daughter of a Moor mother, I felt cheated. I loved you and wanted to marry you. But how could I marry a half-Moor? My Christian faith will never allow me to be happy by going against its tenets."

"Moreover, I thought I was doing it for the good of Christianity just like how you thought fighting a Crusade was for the good of Christianity. I thought I was killing an enemy. I was led to believe by him and your mother that you did not deserve to lead a Christian life because your mother was a Moor!"

"So, I became your enemy, Ralph? We have spent years of our childhood together. We share such beautiful memories of joy and happiness. And yet, a little bit of talk about religion was enough for you to decide to kill me? You could have come to me with my story, couldn't you? "

Then she stopped herself. If she had known that she was part-Moor before she met Haroun, wouldn't she have been ashamed of herself? Wouldn't she have been angry with her father for doing what he did? Sleeping with a Moor woman? Wasn't the meeting with Haroun the life-changing event of her life? Till then, did she know of love in its pure form?

Moreover, how could she be angry with Ralph for choosing to get her killed? She turned inward and asked herself, "Isn't that what I was planning on doing? Joining Captain Philip so I could kill and murder without compunction the likes of Haroun? I went to kill Moors and ended up falling in love with a Moor without even realizing that he was a Moor! And even when I realized the truth about him, my love did not diminish; it only became more passionate because of his ability to be honest and straightforward with me. He did not lie to me to win my love. He only told me the stark truth and let me decide what I wanted to do!"

Wasn't love more powerful than hate? Didn't Jesus Christ also preach love? Did he not say, "Love thy neighbor as much as you love yourself?" Why then do men hate one another so much? Does a man with a burnished skin feel love differently from a man with a white skin?

Gabriella was crying uncontrollably thinking all these thoughts. But deep in her heart, she knew that her father was right. As long as she and Haroun stayed in Mordo, they will be hunted. In the name of religion, these people will not let love to flourish and grow. They will spread hatred. Haroun and she needed to go away. She needed to give her true mother's death a purpose. She needed to love Haroun unconditionally and spread the word of love to all around.

She had no control over wars and battles. But she could control how she lived. She looked across to Haroun. His eyes were filled with her image and he was simply waiting for her to reach out!

She held her hand and he took it and both left the horrible scene through the same tunnel. The last glimpse that people of Mordo had of Gabriella and Haroun was they were riding into the horizon where the sun was rising and bringing hope and light to one and all!